A TOUCH FROM GOD

Freddy Jones

Order this book online at www.trafford.com
or email orders@trafford.com

Most Trafford titles are also available at major online book retailers.

Print information available on the last page.

ISBN: 978-1-4907-6486-3 (sc)
ISBN: 978-1-4907-6490-0 (e)

Trafford rev. 12/15/2015

Trafford
PUBLISHING®   www.trafford.com

North America & international
toll-free: 1 888 232 4444 (USA & Canada)
fax: 812 355 4082

ADVISORY FROM THE AUTHOR

A Touch From God is a fictional story. If any of the events or people in the book sound familiar to you, it is strictly a coincidence.

CHAPTER 1

It was a bright, sunny Sunday morning in May of 1997 when the Johnson family pulled into the parking lot of the Northside Christian Center, a nondenominational, multiethnic church on the north side of Bradenton, Florida.

As the car pulled up to the church, Jason (age 7) and Cindy (age 6), the family's two young children, were having an argument over whose fault it was that the milk spilled at the breakfast table that morning.

Bob, their father, looked up at the rear-view mirror and said, "Jason and Cindy, I want both of you to stop it now!"

Jason argued, "Well, she started it!"

"Did not!" Cindy argued back.

"That's enough out of both of you!" said Kelly, their mother.

"Sometimes I don't know what gets into those two, Kelly," said Bob.

As they walked up the walkway, they spoke and shook hands with a few people, including a tall slender African American man named Tommy Smith, his wife Stephanie, and their three children, Michael, (age 10), Billy, (age 7), and Sally, (age 5).

"Hello, Tommy, how are you doing?" asked Bob.

"Fine, answered Tommy.

"How are the little ones treating you at school?" asked Kelly.

Tommy answered, "Well, you know how it is. It's that time of the year again. The school year is almost over, and the children are acting up because they are starting to get restless."

Kelly responded, "Well, hang in there, it will be over with after a while."

When the family sat down, they greeted more people, including the Martinez family: Carlos, Gloria, his wife, and two of their children, Calvin, (age 8), and Maria, (age 5).

Bob said, "Hello, Carlos. Hello, Gloria. How are you?"

Carlos answered, "Fine. Except we are really worried about Todd, our oldest son. He still wants to go his own rebellious way. He doesn't even want to come to church with us. He says that he thinks that religion is only for weak people and that he knows better than that. Please pray for him. We are very worried about him."

Kelly answered, "We will keep your son in prayer."

"Thank you," Gloria responded.

Soon after that, Nora Wong sat down with her two children, Travis (age 7) and Mary, (age 4), and told them in Chinese that they must sit still and be quiet during the service until the pastor dismissed them for childrens' church. Later, Tommy Smith sat down with his family.

When the service started, the worship leader and the worship team led the congregation in songs like, "Amazing Grace," "Blessed Assurance," "Worthy, You Are Worthy," and "Jesus Is A Firm Foundation." Later, John Donaldson, one of the church leaders, got up to do the announcements. He said, "Please take note of the following announcements: David Kelly is looking for donations for the soup kitchen downtown, the yout group will be having a bake sale to raise money for their missions trip to Jamaica, and please do not forget the big evangelism outreach downtown Friday."

When Pastor Ken Henderson got up to preach, he said, "I have an extra announcement to make. Tyrone Mitchell called me last night and told me that he will not be in church today because he's distressed because he ran over a small child yesterday. The police said it was not his fault, but he is pretty upset and shaken by it. I plan to visit him after church, but I think it would be nice if some of you call him up or visit him and try to encourage him."

When the pastor was making that announcement, Jason giggled a little bit over the thought of someone getting hit by a car, and Kelly smacked him on the hand and said, "Don't laugh at that, it's not funny. You wouldn't think it were funny if it happened to you."

Pastor Henderson dismissed the children for childrens' church, and he started his message.

He said, "Over the past few weeks, I have been ministering on the subject of the working of the Holy Spirit in the Christian Church. However, I sense the need to go away from that subject today and preach a salvation message.

When I talk about salvation, I am not talking about just going to church-even a powerful one like this one, doing good works, having good moral character, or anything else like that. I am talking about having a personal relationship with Jesus Christ. We cannot save ourselves because we can never be good enough to earn God's love or favor, and the Bible tells us that God sees our righteousness as filthy rags. Romans 3:23 states, 'For all have sinned and come short of the glory of God,' and that is why we can never be good enough to save ourselves.

Also, many people try to reach God by means of many religions, but Acts 4:12 warns us that 'Neither is there salvation in any other: for there is none other name under heaven given among men, whereby we must be saved.' That's what the Bible says.

By looking at peoples' faces, a person could tell that the Holy Spirit was moving on the hearts of the people who were listening in the audience as he spoke.

Pastor Henderson went on to say, "Even though we cannot save ourselves, there is hope for us because God promises that if we ask him to forgive us and save us, he will do it. In I John 1:9 it says, 'If we confess our sins, he is faithful and just to forgive our sins and cleanse us from all unrighteousness.'

God promises to forgive us when we ask him to forgive us for sinning against him, and we should forgive people who sin against us."

When the pastor spoke about forgiving others, Kelly looked up at the ceiling and thought about how she had to have a forgiving attitude towards a group of men who broke into her cousin's home and killed him and the rest of his family in 1992. One of the men was shot to death by state troupers and county deputies when he tried to shoot it out with them instead of surrendering to them after a high speed chase that ended on the interstate highway, but the other one surrendered peacefully, and he was sentenced to prison. She also thought about all of the agony that she went through because her cousin was a Godly man and did not deserve to die in such a horrible way. It took months before she was able to get rid of her anger, bitterness, and hatred towards the men who caused her so much grief.

At the same time, Tommy looked down at the church's carpet and thought back on how he had to have a forgiving attitude towards a prejudiced co-worker and a prejudiced manager who tried to do him in when he worked at Jack's Burger Palace when he was younger. Some items had been missing, and the co-worker and the manager tried to pin the thefts on him. Fortunately, a few people stepped forward, told the owner what really happened, and the co-worker and the manager were fired.

Both Kelly and Tommy knew what it was like to be hurt by people, but they also remembered that in the same way that Christ had forgiven them their sins, they should also forgive others when they sin against them.

Pastor Henderson went on to say, "The Gospel of Jesus Christ is meant for everybody, you and those who come in contact with you everyday, and that is why personal evangelism is important. It does not matter what color or race you are, Jesus loves you and wants to come into your heart and life and be your friend. While I am on that, I want to mention that I am happy and blessed to see the great mix of people here as I look at the congregation. I think that it truly represents what the body of Christ is like.

As I conclude, I feel that I must say that Jesus is more than just a great man. He is even more than a great man who did a lot of great things like turning water into wine or healing sick people. He is King of Kings and Lord of Lords, and he wants to be your king and your lord right now if you will let him come in.

Right now, if you have never asked Jesus to come into your heart and life, you may come down to this altar to accept him, and the altar workers will assist you. You may also feel free to come down to the altar if you have any other needs in your life, but please come."

Soon, a crowd of people came down to the altars with their needs. Some of them came to accept Christ as their savior, some of them came to recommit their lives to Jesus, and some of them came to the altar with other needs. Among them were the Johnsons and the Smiths. As Bob and Kelly Johnson waited to get prayer at the altar, Kelly leaned on Bob's right arm around his arm, her eyes closed, and tears ran down her face.

One man who came to the altar for prayer told one of the altar workers, "I have been having some major problems with alcohol addiction, and the trouble that the alcohol has caused me is about to ruin my life and my family. Could you pray for me?"

The altar worker responded, "I can pray for that, but I also want to know if you have given your life to Jesus."

The man responded, "I did that once, but I slipped away from Jesus after a while."

The altar worker smiled and said, "Sir, I will tell you that Jesus will not only take away your drinking problem, he will also save you right here, right now!"

As the altar worker prayed for the man, tears came down the man's face, and he was not only delivered from his alcohol addiction, he was also born again.

At the same time, an altar worker prayed with Carlos and Gloria for their son who was in rebellion against them, and an altar worker prayed with Bob and Kelly for a friend who was very sick.

After the service was over, Carlos and Gloria Martinez briefly spoke with the pastor about the situation with their oldest son, and when they were finished, they walked out of the chapel as they hugged each other with tears in their eyes because they had really been touched by the Lord that day.

CHAPTER 2

It was the afternoon of the day that the nighttime outreach took place when Smith's telephone rang. It was his friend Carlos who called because he did not feel like going to the outreach.

Carlos said, "I know that we have made arrangements for someone to babysit our kids today, but I am about ready to just stay home because of my oldest son."

"What happened?" Tommy asked.

"He told me that he saw nothing wrong with hanging out with his friends and doing drugs, and when I told him that it was wrong, we got into a nasty argument. Before I could say too much, Todd stormed out of the house and slammed the door on me. I just do not know what Gloria and I are going to do about him. It really makes me sad."

Tommy responded, "Well, I understand if that has you upset. Raising a 14-year-old son isn't always easy, especially if he is going through rebellion, but I was looking forward to going on the outreach with you. I'll miss you if you don't come. Listen, I'll pray for you right now."

When Tommy finished praying, Carlos felt better, and he told Tommy that he and his wife would be making the outreach after all.

After Tommy hung up the phone, he went out to his mailbox where he ran into Roy Johnson, his next door neighbor.

Tommy said, "Hi," and Roy said, "Hey, how are you?"

"Fine," Tommy responded.

Roy said, "I think I have seen you around a few times. Aren't you involved with that church that is always doing outreaches where they try to tell people about God around town?"

Tommy smiled and said, "That's right."

Roy frowned and said, "Do you want to know what I think? I think that all of you have flipped! You see, I'm an atheist, and I think that you're a fool to believe in this... this Jesus of yours! I think that religion is just a sham! If there really is a God, then why did he let my sister die from cancer like she did when she was 18? If God cares so much about everything, then how can he let bad things like that happen to people like my sister? She was so young! She didn't deserve to die. Before that happened, I questioned in my mind if there is a God or not, but since that happened, I have been more convinced than ever that there is no God and that religion is only for weak people because they have nothing else to lean on. You and the other people at your church go around sharing your gospel with other people downtown, in jails, nursing homes, and other places, so you can get other people to trust in your Jesus! What a joke!"

Tommy responded, "God is not the one who brings pain and suffering into people's lives, and when the people at my church do outreaches, they are trying to touch peoples' hearts and bring them to Christ because they need him."

Roy frowned and said, "Well, you just keep that stuff to yourself. I don't want to have anything to do with it," and he walked down the street, shaking his head in disgust.

Later on, Tommy and Stephanie joined Bob and Kelly Johnson, Carlos Martinez, and some others for the outreach. While they were at the church, Dick Rose, the outreach leader, went over some instructions and divided the people into groups.

When they arrived downtown for the outreach, some of the people they spoke to were receptive to them, and some were not. Bob and Kelly talked to a man who seemed to feel that he was alright and did not need to accept Christ into his life. When Bob asked him if he knew Jesus, he said, "Well, I think I'm alright. I mean, I'm a good person. I go to church when I can, and I never do things like robbing or killing people. My family is also pretty involved with our church. I usher there, my wife teaches Sunday School for the preschool kids, and my kids are very involved with the youth group. Isn't that good enough?"

Kelly explained to the man that the Bible says that his own personal goodness and good works cannot save him, but even though she and Bob were not able to convince him that he needed to accept Christ in order to be saved, the man let them give him a gospel tract before he left.

When Stan Fogelberg and Sue Stanton tried to share Christ with a group of teen-agers, the teen-agers told them to go away because they did not want to hear it. One of them said, "This is our party night; we don't want to hear that stuff."

Pastor Ken Henderson and outreach leader Dick Rose ran into similar problems when they tried to share the gospel with a rich young couple. When Pastor Henderson tried to start a conversation with them about Christ, the husband in the couple tried to brush them off by saying, "We both have enough money to buy anything we want. We feel secure as we are, and we don't need religion. Besides, there's nothing to religion anyway, and neither of us believe in God."

Nora Wong and the Martinez family had better luck when they ran into a middle-aged man in his fifties. He told them, "It's nice that you go around telling people about God all of the time, but I don't think that there is anything God can do for me. I have messed up my life badly."

Carlos told the man, "It doesn't matter how bad you have had it or what you have done, Christ can save you." (At the time that this conversation was taking place, Nora Wong and Gloria Martinez stood a few feet away as they prayed).

The man responded, "You don't understand. I fought for my country by going to Vietnam where I lost nine of my buddies in a minefield in March of 1971. I survived it by some miracle; it just so happened that I was not close enough to get hurt, but the emotional pain from that was so bad that when I came back home, I messed up my life and my marriage with alcohol and drug abuse. It also hurt when I came off the airline in New York City and had a woman curse me and spit on me instead of thanking me for fighting for my country"

Carlos responded, "I can relate to some of what you are talking to me about. I was still in the United States Army Reserves at the time that the Gulf War broke out in 1991. When my army unit went into battle, it was stressful. It may not have been as bad for me as it was for you, but I saw two of my buddies get seriously wounded in battle, and it hurt me to see that, but by the grace of God I was able to fight in the Gulf War and come home safely.

If you are willing to, I can say a prayer, and you can repeat it after me. If you pray it and mean it, your life will never be the same."

The man agreed to say the sinners' prayer with Carlos, and the man accepted Jesus Christ into his heart as his lord and his savior.

When Carlos finished praying with the man, the man looked at Carlos with a glow on his face and said, "I feel better now. I have been in and out of counseling, but none of it has done this for me."

Tommy and Stephanie had some success when they tried to share the gospel with one man. Even though he said he did not feel like he was ready to give his life to Christ, he did listen to what Tommy and Stephanie had to say, and he let Tommy give him some gospel literature. Before he walked away, he said, "Right now, I feel like I have gained everything. I've been to college, I have a nice job where I am earning more money than I have ever earned in my life, but I still feel like something is missing from my life. Maybe there is something to what you are talking about."

Later, Alfred and Sue Handel, both German immigrants, had success when they shared the Gospel with a very old German woman. When they finished sharing the Gospel with her, she accepted Christ into her heart and life.

At the same time, Ann Wainwright and her sister, Mary, were able to lead an entire family of five, including their three small children to Christ. When the Wainwrights shared the Gospel with the family, the Holy Spirit came on them in a powerful way, and they accepted Christ into their lives right there.

When it was time to stop, everyone assembled together in the parking lot for a brief period of time in which they shared their experiences, and they went home.

When Gloria and Carlos Martinez got home, the babysitter had just put their younger two children to bed, but Todd, their oldest child was not at home.

Carlos asked the babysitter, "Where is Todd?"

The babysitter responded, "I don't know, I haven't seen him since you and Gloria left earlier tonight."

Carlos angrily responded, "He has probably been out on the town this whole time, looking for trouble. That's why I am glad I got you to watch Calvin and Maria. I just cannot depend on him to do anything around here, including watching over his younger brother and sister!"

Seven seconds later, the door burst open, and Todd came in with his mind messed up with marijuana.

When Gloria asked him where he had been, he said, "Oh, just get out of my way and shut up! It's none of your business! Just what is it to you?" and he shoved his mother out of the way as he tried to go up the stairs.

Carlos responded, "You show better respect to her! Don't speak that way to your mother!"

Todd responded, "What's it to you, and just who's gonna make me?" Then he picked up a lamp and tossed it at Carlos, hitting him in the shoulder.

As the trouble started, Calvin and Maria, the Martinez family's younger two children, came out of their rooms because they were frightened.

Gloria shouted, "No children, go back to bed!" in Spanish.

Todd zapped Carlos a few times with his fist, and that is when Gloria dialed 911 for the police.

It was very difficult for Gloria, Carlos, and the babysitter to control Todd because he was very strong and he was messed up from pot.

A few minutes later, three police cars came to the house, and the police ran into the house, restrained Todd, and took him to jail.

When all of this was going on, Calvin and Gloria came out of their rooms again, hugged Gloria, and cried in fright.

Another scuffle started as the policemen tried to get Todd in a patrol car.

After the policemen were finished with Todd, one of them walked over to Carlos and asked him, "Are you alright, sir?"

"Yes, I think I will be okay," Carlos responded.

"Are you sure you won't need any medical assistance? I can call for emergency medical assistance in no time if you need it," the officer said.

"No thanks, I think I will be okay," Carlos responded.

Even though he did not like the idea of pressing charges, he knew that it was the right to do. Soon after that, the police drove away with Todd.

CHAPTER 3

The next morning, Carlos and Gloria discussed the episode that happened with Todd the night before. They were both very upset over the way that it upset their two younger children and the scene that it caused in front of the babysitter. Gloria suggested that they call upon Pastor Henderson, one of the other leaders at the church, or maybe a good close friend for some help and advice about what to do next.

Carlos suggested, "One of us can do that, but if you ask me, I think that he should stay in jail so he can think about what he's done and what he's put us through."

Gloria suggested, "Maybe you or I should call Bob Johnson. He has been very helpful in praying for us in this situation and offering advice on how to deal with Todd."

Carlos phoned Bob, and Cindy, Bob's daughter, answered the phone.

"Hello," answered Cindy.

"Hi, Cindy, this is Mr. Martinez. How are you doing?"

"Fine," answered Cindy.

"Good. Tell me, is your father there?" asked Carlos.

"Just a minute. Daddy, it's for you," said Cindy.

When Bob picked up the phone, Carlos told Bob about what happened the night before with Todd.

"So, where is he now?" asked Bob. "He's still downtown at the jail," answered Carlos.

Bob said, "Well, if you ask me, I think that you should leave him there. You should not have to put up with that. I know that you cannot leave him there forever, but at least for now, he should stay there. I have tried to talk to him, Tommy has tried to talk to him, Pastor Henderson has tried to talk to him, and you have tried to talk to him. Maybe it is time for him to learn that his actions have consequences. You can go out there and bail him out if you want to, but I think you and your family have had to suffer too long with this."

Carlos responded, "I don't think that I or my wife have ever had to face anything like this before. It just seems like too much. Remember, it was just three months ago when my oldest daughter died in a car accident when she was on her way home from visiting a friend. A drunk driver hit her head-on one night, and she died in the hospital the next day. It just doesn't seem fair. She was just sixteen years old."

Bob responded, "I know it's hard, but God allows things like your problems with your son and the death of your daughter to teach us things and to strengthen us. God has a purpose in it. Maybe you and your wife should consider having him go to the drug treatment center. One good place for him might be the Barnabas House because he can not only get treatment for his addiction to drugs, he can also get some spiritual help as well.

Carlos responded, "You know that might be a good idea. My wife and I will pray over that."

Bob prayed for Carlos, his family, and the situation with Todd, and as soon as Bob finished praying and Carlos hung up the phone, the doorbell rang. It was Tommy Smith. Tommy said, "I was on my way to visit Mr. Jake Brown who has been sick and shut in. I just thought that I would stop by on the way and check on you."

Carlos and Gloria told Tommy about the trouble that Todd had caused the night before and how they were thinking of putting him in the Barnabas House Drug Treatment Center. Tommy just sat and listened as they shared their concerns with him. When they finished sharing their concerns with him, he prayed with them for Todd.

When he finished praying, Tommy said, "I have to go now because I want to check on Mr. Brown before it's too late in the day."

"Be careful. I know that the neighborhood he lives in is rough. There are drugs there, there has been violent crime there, and there have been some reports of gangs there," warned Carlos.

When Tommy got to Mr. Brown's house and got out of the car, he ran into a young African American woman who questioned him about his faith. She noticed the Bible in his hand, and she said, "Why do you carry that Bible with you? What are you- saved or something?"

"Yes," said Tommy.

Tommy went on to share his faith with the woman, but when he asked her if she wanted to accept Jesus Christ as her personal savior, she said, "Well, I don't feel like I'm ready yet. I am just not sure that I can commit to that."

Tommy responded, "Jesus will accept you just as you are. You don't have to wait until you feel like you are good enough for him."

The woman smiled and said, "I know that my life is not right, and I need to be saved, but I just don't feel like I can do it right now."

Tommy looked at her with a concerned, serious look on his face and said, "Alright then, but please don't wait until it is too late," and he handed her a small Red Bible.

When Tommy knocked on Mr. Brown's door, a tall, friendly Jamaican man came to the door. It was Mr. Brown.

Tommy stayed at Mr. Brown's house for a good while. They laughed and shared some nice stories with each other, and Tommy prayed for Mr. Brown before he left.

Just as Tommy left Mr. Brown's house, one man was making threats against another man. The man who was getting the threats ran away as the other man pulled out a gun and began firing at him. Before Tommy could duck or do anything else to get out of the way, two stray bullets hit him. One of them hit him in the side of the head, and the other one hit him on the arm. Tommy lay on the ground, half-dead.

CHAPTER 4

Within minutes, a huge crowd gathered where Tommy was shot, and someone placed a call to the 911 emergency center for help. Mr. Brown ran out to see what was going on, and when he saw Tommy bleeding heavily as he lay flat on the ground, he ran back into his house to call Tommy's wife.

Meanwhile, the police arrived, and EMS and fire department personnel arrived soon after. Mr. Brown helplessly stood over Tommy, and he cried while the EMS workers frantically worked to save Tommy's life and as additional policemen came to the scene.

When Stephanie arrived and saw what had happened, all she could do was cling to Mr. Brown and cry.

Mr. Brown angrily said, "Who would want to do a terrible thing like this to such a nice man? He never did anything to hurt anybody!"

The firemen and EMS workers decided that the best thing to do to save Tommy's life would be to have him airlifted to the closest trauma center. A half hour later, a chopper arrived near the scene and airlifted Tommy to a trauma center in nearby St. Petersburg.

Tommy's wife felt horrible about having to go to her sister's house where her children had stayed the night before so she and Tommy could go to the downtown outreach the night before and also so her sister could take them to the beach that day and have to tell them that someone had shot their father. She walked up to the doorstep of her sister's house, trembling and crying.

When her sister answered the doorbell and saw the shocked state that Stephanie was in, she asked, "What's wrong, Stephanie?"

With a quiver in her voice, Stephanie told her sister and her three children what had happened.

Stephanie's sister, Anna, covered her mouth as she displayed a shocked look on her face, and they hugged each other and wept.

Stephanie asked Anna, "Would it be okay with you if I had my children stay with you for another night?"

Anna said, "Definitely. It will be no problem. Just get more of the kids' clothes, and I can keep them for you. Just be careful, especially on that Skyway Bridge. It would also be a good idea if you took someone with you on that trip and not go up there alone."

Sally shouted, "No, Mommy, we want to come with you!" but Stephanie told her that she must do this alone and that she (Sally) would be better off at her aunty's house.

Before she left, she hugged her three children, she asked her sister, Anna, to call Pastor Henderson and some of the family's closest friends, and let them know what happened.

One of the families that Anna called was the Johnson family. When their phone rang, Kelly answered it, and when the phone call was over, Kelly walked away from the phone with her hand over her mouth and tears in her eyes.

Jason asked, "What's wrong, Mommy?" and Bob asked, "Honey, what's wrong?"

"T-T-Tommy's been s-sh-shot, and he may not survive," Kelly said tearfully.

When Kelly told her family about what happened to Tommy, they cried.

Bob said tearfully, "The two things that Tommy and his family need right now are our prayers and our support," and the Johnson family prayed for the Smiths as they held hands together.

Word quickly spread about what happened to Tommy, and people kept Tommy and his family in their prayers. Meanwhile, Tommy lay unresponsive and clinging to his life at the trauma center.

For three weeks, Tommy's wife, Stephanie, and Tommy's parents, Jeff and Katie Smith, visited Tommy, and they sat by his side because they were hoping and praying for a miracle for him.

The main concern that Tommy's doctors had was the damage that the bullet wound to Tommy's head would cause. When Tommy first arrived at the trauma center, the bullet that hit him in the head had broken into small pieces, but miraculously, the bullet pieces disappeared.

Even though Tommy still lay unresponsive in the hospital room after he was shot, it just seemed to go against what is natural and normal for the bullet to disappear like it did. All of the doctors knew that it had to be a miracle. One of the doctors who performed the operation on Tommy's arm and head exclaimed, "I cannot explain this, but I just cannot find any bullet pieces here!"

For three weeks, Tommy continued to cling to his life with the use of the breathing equipment by his hospital bed. It was the middle of June then, and while many other people were making vacation plans, Stephanie was still spending much time visiting Tommy at the trauma center.

In between visiting her sick husband and trying to keep things going at home, Stephanie received much encouragement and support from her family and friends, including the Martinez family, a family that was also going through a struggle. Their teen-age son was still rebelling, but even though that was not easy to deal with, Carlos and Gloria did not let it keep them down or stop them from reaching out to the Smiths. They did manage to get Todd to go to the Barnabas House Drug Rehabilitation Center, but it was not easy with Todd because Todd's heart was hard and he often gave the people who tried to work with him at Barnabas House a hard time. Todd did let his parents put him there, but he only let them do it to get them off his back, not because he wanted to change. He was still just as tough and rebellious as ever. Still yet, Carlos and Gloria still took time out to minister to Stephanie and her children with sympathy cards and phone calls, and it really helped Stephanie to feel like she could face her tough situation.

CHAPTER 5

The situation stayed the same for a long time, and it seemed as if things were not going to get any better until the morning of July 1, 1997 when Stephanie received a phone call from Dr. Horne, the head doctor who cared for Tommy. When Stephanie answered the phone, he told her, "I was in Tommy's room when he became responsive again and he asked for you! He is conscious now, but he is still very weak and still has a long way to go."

Stephanie's face glowed with joy when she got the news, and she said, "Praise the Lord!"

She quickly got her children fed and dressed so she could leave them at her sister's house while she visited her husband. She was so happy and excited that she forgot to tell her children the good news about Tommy! When they were eating, Michael, her oldest child asked, "Why are you rushing us, Mom?"

Stephanie came back to her senses and told Michael, Billy, and Sally that their dad was beginning to feel better again. Her children yelled, "Yay!" "Yippie!" and "Goody!" but Stephanie had to explain to them that their father was still in pretty bad shape, and because they were so young, they could not visit where their father was. They moaned a little bit, but they basically understood.

Everything went smoothly until the children got into the car. When Michael got into the car, he accidentally shoved into Sally, and she said, "Stop it, Michael, or I'm talling the tops on you!" (She was really trying to say, "Stop it, Michael, or I'm calling the cops on you!")

Michael said, "I didn't do anything!" and Stephanie said, "That's enough out of both of you-now stop it!"

Stephanie drove up to Anna's house, and Anna just happened to be in the driveway to get her mail. When Stephanie told her the good news about Tommy, Anna shouted,

"Praise God!" and she hugged Stephanie. They both cried tears of joy because of the good news, and Sally asked, "Why are you crying, Mommy?"

Stephanie answered, "I am crying because I am happy for your daddy. People don't just cry when they hurt themselves or feel sad, they also cry when they are happy."

Before she left to go to the trauma center in St. Petersburg, she called Tommy's parents to let them know about Tommy, and Tommy's father, Jeff, told her that he and his wife had already received the good news from Tommy's doctor.

Stephanie drove to St. Petersburg with Tommy's parents like she did before, and Dr. Horne met them when they got to the hospital waiting room.

Dr. Horne said, "I understand how anxious you are to see Tommy. This morning, Tommy opened his eyes for the first time since the incident, and he is responsive now. However, I must tell you that Tommy is still very weak, and he has a long way to go. He is going to need your support now more than ever.

Jeff responded, "Well, there is no doubt that we are going to do that," and his wife, Katie, nodded her head in agreement.

Dr. Horne added, "You seem to be a religious family, and it seems that your faith is helping you through this. He is going to need all of the prayer, love, and support that you can give him. I say, whatever you have been doing to get through this, just keep on doing it."

As they walked to Tommy's hospital room, Katie and Jeff briefly used the moments they had to share how their Christian faith was helping them get through the rough times that they were facing. When they reached Tommy's room, Dr. Horne smiled and said, "That's great. That's beautiful."

Since Tommy could only have two visitors at a time, Tommy's parents, Jeff and Katie, went to see him first. They walked over to where Tommy was with tears in their eyes and leaned over Tommy's bed.

"How are you doing, honey?" asked Katie, and Tommy weakly replied, "Fine."

Tommy asked, "Did they ever find out who did this to me?" and Jeff answered, "Yes, soon after it happened, they arrested a man named James Little and charged him with the crime. They are keeping him at the county jail.

Tommy's parents spoke a little longer with him, but they tried to keep it short because they knew that Tommy was still very weak, and they wanted to let him see Stephanie.

When Stephanie went in to see Tommy, he gave her a weak smile. He was awake and responsive, but he did look frail, weak, and wasted away.

Stephanie shed a few tears and placed her hand on his arm. Then she asked, "How are you doing, honey?"

"Fine," replied Tommy with a weak voice.

Stephanie added, "A lot of people have been praying for you and asking about you. We have been getting phone calls from people whom we don't know but are still offering prayers and support for you. Even our two close friends, Carlos and Gloria, who even though they have been going through a rough time with their son, have reached out to us."

"How are the kids?" asked Tommy.

"They are fine. They keep asking if you are going to be back home soon, but I have to tell them that you are too weak for that. They have also been praying for you. Here, here's a picture that Sally drew. It is a picture of the family."

Stephanie handed the picture to Tommy, and Tommy took a look at it. Tommy smiled and said, "Hey, she's quite an artist."

They both spoke a few more minutes, but Stephanie tried to cut the conversation short because she remembered that Tommy was still very weak.

After Tommy's wife and parents left, Tommy fell asleep. He did not wake up again until Mary King, one of the nurses, came to check his blood pressure. She asked him, "How are ya?" and he smiled and said, "Fine" with a weak voice.

When the nurse left, he had his private daily devotional time of prayer and Bible study. He knew he wasn't in any shape to kneel down beside his hospital bed, but he also knew that it didn't matter to God.

After dinner, Tommy had one of the nurses sit him up a little bit so he could look out of the window and think. As he looked out of the window, he could see that it was nightfall, and he checked out the bright lights from the city around him. Looking out of the window, he could imagine that there were things happening; parents were putting their children to bed, people were going out to dinner, people were working, people were making shopping trips, people were visiting friends, and people were just going on with their lives in other ways. He began to think about the long road to recovery that lay before him before he could get back to living a normal life again. Tommy knew that he should not hold resentment, bitterness, or anger against the person who shot him, but he could not help thinking about how tough this person had made life for him. Here he lay in a hospital bed as he wondered when or if he would ever be able to live a normal, decent life again while the person who shot him had full use of his muscle and body movements even though he had to stay in jail.

Tommy also began to worry about how he was going to be able to provide for his family because of this; would he ever be able to see the day when he could teach again, or would he have to live off disability for the rest of his life? How was he going to send his children off to college? How was he going to pay off the family bills, especially the medical bills from his stay at the hospital, the ride in the emergency chopper, and the cost from the EMS workers?

Along with that, Tommy began to think about his family, his friends, and his church back home; What were his wife and children doing now? How were Carlos and Gloria dealing with Todd's drug abuse and rebellion? What would the Fourth of July be like since he could not spend it with his family? Sure he could probably watch the fireworks from his hospital room because he had such a high view of the city, but it would not be the same without his family. Still yet, other thoughts began to go through his mind as he lay in the hospital bed.

Just then, something supernatural and powerful began to happen. God's presence and the peace of Christ began to fill the hospital room in a very powerful way. The Holy Spirit came upon Tommy, and he began to cry. In a normal or natural situation, Tommy could not cry. It was not that Tommy was too hard or too proud to cry, he just had a hard time doing it. Even if he were hurting, he would cry on the inside, not on the outside. However, this was not a usual situation. As God's presence and the Peace of Christ filled the room, Tommy began to feel better; he felt like Jesus was telling him, "Trust me, and it will be alright. I'm your best friend, and I will see you through this." Instantly, he was reminded of a part of Isaiah 43:5 which reads, "Fear not: for I am with thee...," and he began to feel like everything was going to be alright because the Lord was with him. Tommy was 34-years-old, and he had been saved since he was 14, but he had never felt anything like this before. He knew that he would never be the same again because of this experience. Likewise, he felt like he had found new courage to go on.

CHAPTER 6

Weeks passed, and Tommy's condition continued to improve. Everyone, including the doctor who worked with Tommy, knew that it had to be a miracle the way that Tommy was improving; they knew that in the natural, people either do not survive gunshot wounds to the head, take a longer time to recover from them, or wind up having to live the rest of their lives unable to take care of themselves. Yet, Tommy was miraculously recovering by the week!

Pastor Henderson, his wife, his parents, and a few other people from his church made the trip to the trauma center to visit and encourage Tommy. Tommy also received many cards and letters from people who were from his church, people who knew him at Carter Elementary School, and people who just knew from around town. On one visit, Pastor Henderson told him, "I have always appreciated your childlike faith in the Lord. I think that it is really going to get you through this."

On August 1, Doctor Horne told Tommy that his improvement was so good that he was going to be able to transfer to Johnson Hospital in Bradenton to complete his recovery.

Tommy was overjoyed at the news, but he did not know that not only was his move to Johnson Hospital in Bradenton going to put him a step closer in his recovery, it was also going to be a time when God was going to do a powerful work in his life.

On August 10, 1997, an air ambulance flew Tommy from St. Petersberg to Sarasota. When the air ambulance landed in Sarasota, Tommy's family, his parents, Pastor Henderson, a group of paramedics, and a local sheriff's deputy met Tommy for the trip from the airport to the hospital. When the small group of vehicles left the airport, t.v. news crews followed not far behind them and filmed some of it.

When Tommy arrived at Johnson Hospital, he felt like he was halfway finished with his recovery even though he knew deep down that he still had a long way to go.

Before he went to his hospital room, the doctors at the hospital let him spend a few minutes with his parents, Pastor Henderson, and his family. It was the first time since the shooting that he got to see his children, and they gave him a big hug. The day went fast. Dr. Judah Goldman, the head doctor who would be caring for Tommy, gave Tommy, Tommy's family, Pastor Henderson and his wife, and Tommy's parents some briefing on how he was going to care for Tommy.

In the coming weeks, Tommy made some amazing recovery under Judah Goldman's care, but God planned to give Tommy more than just a physical miracle: God planned a spiritual miracle also. Almost on a daily basis, people who knew Tommy came by and visited him.

One week after Tommy came to Manatee memorial Hospital, David Smith, the principal at Carter Elementary School, the school where Tommy worked, came by to see Tommy.

He shook Tommy's hand and said, "How are you doing?"

"Fine," answered Tommy.

"I just want to let you know that we appreciate you and your hard work at Carter Elementary. You work well with the other staff and faculty members, and you are great with the kids. The whole school supports you and loves you.

I know that you will not be able to come in and start the new school year next week, but we are praying and hoping that you will be back again with us someday," said David Smith.

David continued, "Anytime that you want to talk to me about your faith, I am willing to listen. Just come to my office, and we can talk about it. I think it is wonderful how your faith has brought you through this."

Later, and on the same day, Carlos Martinez, Tommy's close friend, came to see him. Carlos hugged him and said, "Hey, Tommy, how are ya, buddy?"

Tommy responded, "Fine. I think I'm feeling better now. Hey, have things gotten any better with your oldest son, Todd?"

Carlos shook his head and said, "Not like I would like to see. I mean, things do seem to be improving with him, but it seems to be very slow and gradual. Sometimes he acts like he is going backwards, but he is getting away from drugs and his old druggy buddies. We're just praying that he will get totally delivered from his drug lifestyle and turn to Christ.

"That's good," Tommy said with a serious look on his face.

Carlos smiled and said, "Hey, I came to check on you and see how you are doing. I did not come to whine about my problems!"

"Well, I do feel a lot better now than I did when I was in St. Petersburg, but I don't know when I will be able to go home and be back with my family again. I have really been through a lot," answered Tommy.

"I know," said Carlos. Tommy added, "I don't know why I am going through all of this. I'm not sure if all of this happened by chance, or if it is some test that God has allowed to come into my life to teach me something."

Carlos put in, "I think it is probably the latter with the way it happened. Look, I don't think I should stay here too long because I know that you need rest. I just thought that I would stop by and let you know that we are praying for you. I appreciate the way you reached out to me and my family when we first came here from Texas. We did not know anybody here, but you befriended us. I know that it probably took some effort on your part because you are not an outgoing person, but you still took the time and the effort to befriend us."

"Hey, I'll keep Todd in my prayers," said Tommy.

Carlos smiled, gave Tommy the thumbs up sign, and left.

A half-hour later, Charity McDonald, a young Irish woman whom Tommy had known since fourth grade, came by to visit him. Tommy smiled and he looked surprised when he saw her come in.

"Hey, Tommy, how have you been?" asked Charity.

"Fine, but I don't know how much longer I will have to stay here."

Charity added, "I'm glad to see that you are feeling better now. I just came by to tell you that I appreciate the way that you have been such a friend to me through all of these years. I still remember how you befriended me when my family moved here from Ireland. I was just nine years old.

Remember, some of the kids made fun of me because of my Irish accent and because of speech problems that came from a near-fatal car accident that I was in when

I was just a four-year-old child living in Ireland. You made me feel like I had a friend when you and two other students reached out to me, and I felt better for it. You did the same thing later on in junior high school, and because of the way that you befriended me, I accepted Jesus Christ as my personal savior. Because of your love, compassion, and the way that you told me about Christ, my life is different now. I know I didn't accept Christ right away- I said I would think about it. Now I am glad that I made the decision to accept Christ.

I have a family with two small girls now, but I don't work in a career now. I feel that my most important job now is raising my three and six-year-old daughters now. Still, I feel that I am worth something now because of Jesus. I don't have to feel like I'm a nobody. Well, I cannot stay long, but I thought that it would make you feel better if I came by and told you about the influence you have had on my life."

Charity hugged Tommy and waved to him before she left.

The encouraging words that Carlos and Charity spoke to Tommy stayed with him for the rest of the day, but the encouraging words were not over yet.

At 7:00 that night, Peter Johnson, a young African American man whom he had known since he was involved in his church's youth group as a teen-ager, came back to see him.

When he came into the room, he shook Tommy's hand and asked how he was. Yet, what really stood out to Tommy was the encouraging words that he gave Tommy when he said, "I just came by to say, 'thank you' for reaching out to me the way you did when we were in the Spiritual Warriors Youth Group. When I first came there, I felt left out because I didn't feel like I fit in there, and I remember that you also felt that way. Yet, you still took the time to reach out to me and a few other people who felt left out and forgotten.

Remember, I gave my life to Jesus because you cared enough to reach out to me. I am now a childrens' pastor at Covenant Assembly of God in Sarasota where I am putting into practice with children what you taught me when we were both teen-agers. Well, I have to go now. I can't stay too long. It's just that I saw what happened to you on the news a few months ago, and when I found out that you are feeling better, I thought I would come by and encourage you."

Peter shook Tommy's hand before he left, and he said, "I and the children in the Genesis Childrens' Church at my church have been praying for you. Get well. You're a good man!" As Peter walked out of the room, he gave Tommy the 'I love you' sign.

In a little while, it was going to be nightfall, but Tommy just could not forget the words that Carlos, Charity, and Peter spoke to him. It was as if it were no coincidence that they came by to visit him. Still yet, there would be more soon. As Tommy went to sleep that night, he still could not get their words out of his mind.

CHAPTER 7
_____

The next day, Tommy woke up thinking about the three visits he had the day before. He knew that it was God's way of encouraging him during his dark time and God's way of getting him to look at something else besides his bad situation.

Tommy also thought of the fact that it was Sunday morning and that he could not be at church with his family and friends. Since it was Sunday, he thought he would see few or no visitors that day, but Tommy was wrong. The ministry that God had been doing and had started with Tommy the day before was not over with yet.

Later in the day, Thelma Anderson, a short, African American woman who knew Tommy since he was a child in elementary school, stopped by to visit him. She walked into the room, gave Tommy a hug, and asked him, "How are you doin,' sweetie?"

Tommy smiled and said, "Fine."

Thelma said, "I know you haven't forgotten me, your old tutor in elementary school! You were just a little thing in second grade, and you were having trouble with your reading skills. I tutored you, I believed in you, and look how far you've come! I just knew that the Good Lord was going to pull you through because I prayed for you. You have always been special to me ever since you were a little child in second grade. God is not finished with you yet. You just keep holding on, and don't let anybody tell you that you can't make it!"

As if that were not enough, within an hour after Thelma Anderson left, Erick Gonitski, an outgoing and outspoken grandson of Polish immigrants, came to the hospital with his wife, Lisa, and 13-year-old daughter, Tracey, to see him. When they walked through the door, Erick and Lisa shook hands with him, and Erick asked him how he was doing.

"Fine," Tommy responded.

Erick said, "I am glad to see that you are feeling better, and I have really enjoyed getting to know you since you came to Northside Christian Center." Erick's wife and daughter did not say anything at first. Tracey smiled and winked at him while Lisa smiled and squeezed Tommy on his arm.

Erick added, "I admire the courage that you and your family have shown through this whole thing. It has really been a testimony. It has really been a testimony to the whole congregation."

Lisa added, "Too many times, people get angry or bitter and shake their fists at God when they go through things like this, but it seems like it has drawn your family closer to God and closer together. I think that that is powerful."

Tommy responded, "Well, it has not been totally easy for us ever since I was shot. There have been those times when I have felt like I wanted to doubt God and ask him, 'Why, why did it have to happen?' but my family's faith in Jesus has kept us strong and seen us through this. I don't think that we would have held on without him."

"Well, just remember that the Bible tells us that the trials and the tribulations that we face here on earth do not compare to what it will be like when we spend eternity with Jesus. Just think, it hasn't been easy for you lately, but one day you and I will stand side by side with many, many others so we can meet Jesus face to face and spend eternity with him.

One day, your family, my family, and many, many others will be able to spend eternity with Jesus, enjoying his presence and praising him. We won't have to deal with things like this anymore!" said Erick.

Before they left, Lisa reminded him of Psalm 34:19 which reads, "Many are the afflictions of the righteous: but the Lord delivereth him out of them all."

Still yet, it did not end with the Gonitskis. A short time after Tommy ate dinner, Billy Brown, a young African American man in his thirties, came by to visit him. When he stopped by, he said, "I heard about what happened to you back in May, and I have been following it on the news. I just thought that I would come by and take the time now to thank you for helping me to learn how to read. I know that I have thanked you before, but I just want to thank you again. Back a few years ago, I was illiterate, and I could not get a good job, but shortly after I got saved, I came to you because I wanted to be able to read the Bible.

You and your wife took the time to tutor me twice a week so I could learn how to read, and now my life is different. I can't even begin to tell you of the joy that I get from reading the Bible to myself without having to have my wife read it to me. I love it, and I also enjoy reading Bible stories to my children.

Now that I can read, I have a better chance of getting a good job. I recently applied to get a job at a big department store, and my wife and I are praying that I will get it if it's God's will."

Tommy smiled and said, "Well, that is nice to hear. I hope that you do get that job. I think that life will be better for you now that you can read."

Before he left, the man said, "Hang in there, man. We're praying for you."

As Tommy went to sleep that night, he thought back on what had happened to him that day and the day before. There was not a doubt in his mind then that God was trying to comfort him in his time of trouble, and he knew that God was using friends and people whom he had ministered to in the past to do it. However, there seemed to be more to it than that. It seemed as if God was using this situation to shower him with love and show him how special he was to God. It was not that Tommy was anymore special to God than anyone else. It was just that God was using this experience to show him how special he was to him. For a long time, Tommy knew that God could lift a person up when a person is down, but he was getting to feel and experience it for himself this time.

A few days passed, and Tommy did not get any visits from people like the people who had visited him before. He did get few visits from his wife and parents and a phone call from the pastor, but except for that, he didn't get any visits. It was Wednesday, October 1, now, and school had been in session for at least a month then. Before he went out for a stroll in his wheelchair, he sat and looked through the get well letters and cards he had received from children and adults he knew from work and church.

As he wheeled himself down the hallway, he wondered how things were going at the elementary school where he worked. Just then, an old man wheeled himself up to Tommy and said, "Hello there, young fellow. I just wanted to tell you that I heard about what happened to you and that I admire your courage and strength."

Tommy looked at the man and said, "Thanks."

The man shook Tommy's hand and said, "My name is Sam-Sam Stone."

Tommy said, "My name is Tommy Smith."

"I already know who you are," Sam said with a smile.

Sam asked, "Are you a Christian?"

"Yes I am," answered Tommy.

"I am too," said Sam.

Sam added, "I have seen the way people have reached out to you and the faith that your family has, and it's really touching. Ever since I had my car accident, I have had people treat me the same way, but I just admire the way that people have reached out to you."

"That's nice to hear," said Tommy.

After they wheeled themselves to the waiting room, they sat and talked for a while until lunchtime.

Just before they went to their rooms to eat, they saw a woman walking down the hall with her five-year-old son and six-year-old daughter. She had just come out of the hospital room where she visited her husband, but Tommy and Sam wondered how she managed to get children who were that young into a patient's room, since children that young were not allowed in.

However, that was just the point: a doctor had nicely told her that he would let it go this time but that she could not make a habit of it because it was not allowed.

When she and her two young children walked down the hall, the boy said, "Mommy, let's stop at the gift shop!"

The boy's mother responded, "I'm sorry, honey, but we cannot go now. We have to go home now because the t.v. repairman is coming this afternoon."

"I wanna go to the gift shop!" screamed the boy, and threw a nasty tantrum. Several nurses and an orderly looked to see what was going on when they heard the screaming.

The mother quickly gave in and said, "Alright honey, we can stop at the gift shop if you really want to go there," and they left.

Tommy and Sam looked at the whole scene with upset looks on their faces.

Tommy commented, "I can't believe what I just saw."

Sam added, "That's the trouble with a lot of children today-no discipline! If that had been my young'un, he wouldn't have been able to sit down for a week when I got finished with him!"

Tommy said, "My daughter is strongwilled. She tried that with me several times. I dealt with her sternly each time she did it. Now she doesn't do it anymore."

One of the nurses who saw the whole thing shook her head in disgust as she went back to work.

A few hours had passed, Sam was in his room with two old friends who came to visit him, and Tommy was wheeling himself into the waiting room when he got another encouraging visit. It was Bob Johnson and his family.

Bob shook Tommy's hand and said, "Hey Tommy, how are you?"

"Fine," responded Tommy.

Kelly said, "Bob and I were going to each take turns going in your room to see you so one of us could be here in the waiting room to watch the kids. Is it alright if we just meet here?"

"Sure it is," answered Tommy.

Bob asked, "Have you been hanging in there alright?"

Tommy responded, "Yes. It seems like I have been getting better now by the week."

Kelly commented, "Well, you just keep hanging in there, and it'll get better after a while."

Just then, Jason, the Johnson family's 7-year-old son, walked up to Tommy and said, "Look, I got a good citizen award at school Friday, and check out my cool baseball cards!"

Tommy smiled and said, "That's nice. Do you like baseball?"

"Yeah. Dad and I really like this baseball team," answered Jason.

Cindy, the Johnson family's 6-year-old daughter, walked over to Tommy, pointed to her feet and said, "Look, my mommy bought me these nice sneakers."

Tommy smiled and said, "Wow, they are pretty! Hey, why are all of you so dressed up?"

Kelly answered, "We were on our way home from visiting a friend and we thought we would stop by to see you and tell you how much we love and appreciate you."

Bob looked at Tommy, nodded his head, and said, "We thought it would encourage you if we let you know how special you are to us. We love getting to know you and have you as a friend."

Before they left, Bob and Kelly hugged Tommy, and Kelly said, "We love you. You get better now, you hear?"

As the Johnson family walked away, their two young children looked back and waved at Tommy. Then, they both turned back, ran over to Tommy, and they gave him a big hug. Bob smiled, and Kelly shed a tear because she was so touched to see her children learn to show compassion at such young ages. Then, Jason and Cindy went back to their parents and left. It didn't even matter to Tommy that Jason and Cindy were just small children because it was through that single act of kindness and love that God showed him that he can use anybody to minister to someone.

Still yet, it did not end with that. The next day, Tommy was sitting on the edge of his bed, watching television, when his cousin, Allen, and Allen's wife, Sophia, walked in. It was the first time that they saw him since he was transported from the trauma center in St. Petersburg to Johnson Hospital in Bradenton.

When they both walked in, they hugged him, and Allen said, "I see a lot of improvement in you since we saw you in St. Petersburg. How do you feel?"

"I feel a lot better now," answered Tommy.

"We're glad to hear that," responded Sophia.

"I really appreciate your coming all the way down to see me. I know that it's a long drive from Tallahassee to Bradenton, and you still have the long drive back," said Tommy.

"That's no problem. We just had to come and see how you were doing when we heard that you are improving. Besides, we've arranged to spend the night at your parents' house before we go back to Tallahassee," answered Sophia.

Sophia said, "The distance is no big deal. It's just that we love you, and when you love somebody, the distance doesn't really matter.

Allen put in, "I know that we mainly came here to see if you are feeling better, but that's not the only reason we came here. We came here to tell you that we appreciate you and the way that you reached out to us when we were married. Remember, when we first got married, we caught a little bit of flack from some people just because we have an interracial marriage. We've even had Christians or people who call themselves Christians say unkind things about us or to us, and it is just because Sophia is a Spaniard and I am African American. Yet, you and some other people from your church reached out to us and supported us through that. You and a few other people at your church showed us that in every part of life, including marriage, it isn't race or color that matters because Jesus is what matters. I know that even though you don't see anything wrong with interracial relationships, you personally choose not to go that way because of the pressure against it. Yet, you never let it keep you from reaching out to us, and that has really ministered to us."

"Good. I am glad to hear that," Tommy responded.

Tommy, Allen, and Sophia talked a little while longer until it was time to go.

A few hours later, Tommy was sitting in his wheelchair again and looking out of his window when he got another visitor. This time it was his wife, Stephanie.

"Hi, how are ya?" asked Stephanie as she gave Tommy a hug.

"Fine," answered Tommy.

"Good! What have you been up to?" asked Stephanie.

"Well, I've just been sitting here, looking out at the city and thinking," responded Tommy.

"Well, before you get too interested or too bored with that, I have a surprise waiting out in the waiting room for you," Stephanie said.

"What is it? Tommy asked.

"You'll have to come and see," replied Stephanie.

When Stephanie wheeled Tommy's wheelchair into the waiting room, she and Tommy saw their three children, Michael, Billy, and Sally, and Stephanie's sister, Anna.

When the children saw Tommy, they ran towards him and yelled, "Daddy!"

It was the first time since the shooting that Tommy really got to spend quality time with his kids. It was true that he got to see them for a few moments when he first came back to Bradenton, but it was very brief. This time it would be different. Now, he could spend as much time as he wanted to for loving on his kids.

As his children grouped around him, they seemed to be competing against each other for his attention because they were so eager to talk to him. Stephanie, Anna, and a nearby nurse just stood by and smiled, but Tommy said, "Hey, hey, whoa, wait a minute! I love all of you, but I can only hear one of you at a time!"

Just then, Anna intruded into the confusion that was going on by giving him a big hug and saying, "How are ya? It's so good to see you again."

"Are you gonna come home now, Daddy?" asked Sally.

"I'm not sure when I will be back home again, but I do hope that it's soon, honey," Tommy said as he kissed her on the cheek.

"Guess what, Daddy! I got an 'A' on my spelling test last week!" injected Billy.

Tommy responded, "Hey, that is nice! I am proud of you!" and gave Billy a high-five.

Michael has something special to tell you, too," said Stephanie.

"I am going to be Gabriel in the Christmas play in December," said Michael.

"They just started casting for the Christmas program, and they felt that he would be good for the part," said Stephanie.

As the time passed, Tommy talked and laughed with Anna and his family. Just a little while before the visiting hours were over, Dr. Judah Goldman and Nurse Cathy Fields came into the room to check on Tommy.

Dr. Goldman said, "Well, I see you're feeling better now! Maybe now you're ready for us to check your blood pressure and take another blood sample right now."

Tommy said, "Hey, wait a minute. Maybe I am not that much better!"

Everybody laughed when they heard Tommy say that, and it felt good to have some light humor in such a tough situation.

CHAPTER 8

The next day, Stephanie left her children at Anna's house so she could spend some time with Carlos and Gloria. She just felt that since the situation with Todd had not gotten much better, she would take some time to minister to Carlos and Gloria.

When Stephanie approached the door, Gloria said, "Hi Stephanie, how have you been?"

"Fine, how are you?" replied Stephanie.

"Fine, but this is a surprise!" said Gloria.

Stephanie responded, "Well, I just don't feel good about rejoicing over my own situation's getting better when I know that your situation has not."

"Well, that's nice. That's awfully kind of you. We appreciate that," said Carlos.

"So, how has Todd been? Has there been any change with him?" asked Stephanie.

"There has been some change, but it hasn't been much. He will sit through counseling now, and he will listen to Bible teaching, but he still hasn't come to the place where he will change from his druggie lifestyle and make Jesus the lord of his life," answered Carlos.

Gloria added, "It is a change that he will listen to a presentation of the Gospel and listen to counseling, but he still hasn't taken it to heart like we want him to."

"Well, I'm praying for Todd. Even though I've been going through a lot, I still remember Todd as well as Tommy in my prayers," Stephanie said as she patted Gloria on the arm.

"Well, thanks," replied Gloria.

"Any prayer is helpful," added Carlos.

Just then, the telephone rang. It was Todd. Carlos picked it up.

"Hello," said Carlos.

"Hi, this is Todd. Is this Dad?" asked Todd.

"Yes, what's up?" Carlos asked.

Todd answered, "I have good news for you. I have turned away from drugs, and I've given my life to Christ!"

"Well, praise God! I'm glad to hear that!" Carlos responded.

Todd added, "I began to think about what happened to Mr. Smith, and it made me think about my own life. I began to see how precious, fragile, and unpredictable life can be. You can be just going along, minding your own business, and your life can be snatched away in an instant. You can't just keep living any kind of way that you want to as if you can do it forever. You have to make sure that your life is right with God and do it now, before it's too late."

"Amen. I am glad to hear that. Hey, would you like to tell your mother about this?" asked Carlos.

"Yes," answered Todd.

"Hello Todd, what's up?" asked Gloria as she picked up the phone.

Todd answered, "Well, first of all, I want to apologize for the way that I was living before I came to this Christian drug treatment center. I know that I haven't been very pleasant here either, but after a while I began to think about how Mr. Smith almost lost his life. If life is that uncertain, then I need something that I can depend on. So, last night I talked with Rick Daniels, one of the counselors here, and I gave my life to Jesus. I don't think that I will ever be the same again. I don't need drugs or any of the other garbage that the Devil has to offer me."

Gloria began to sob, and she said, "Praise the Lord! You don't know how long we have been praying for that! I just rejoice that you have finally come to know Jesus!"

Carlos and Gloria spoke to Todd from different phones for a little while longer, and they hung up.

When the phone conversation was over, Gloria turned to Stephanie and said, "That was Todd. He gave his life to Jesus last night!"

"Amen! I am glad to hear that," responded Stephanie.

"We did not mean to be rude to you by talking so long on the phone, but we are just so happy now that our oldest son is saved! Praise the Lord!" said Carlos with excitement in his voice.

"That's alright. I understand. I rejoice with you. Two miracles have happened now. I know that Tommy will be happy to hear about this!" said Stephanie.

Soon after that, Stephanie left the Martinez house and went to Johnson Hospital to visit Tommy and tell him about Todd. However, when she got there, she had an unpleasant surprise. Before she could even reach Tommy's hospital room, she ran into Dr. Goldman who told her that Tommy had taken a bad turn.

"I need to let you know that Tommy has somehow contracted pneumonia, and we are watching him closely," stated Dr. Goldman.

"But...but how? I don't understand. He was doing so well yesterday when I visited him. What happened?" Stephanie said with a hint of worry in her voice.

"I am not sure. One thing that I do know is that now that we are in the middle of October and the temperature is dropping, it is easier now for people to catch cold-weather related sicknesses. I know that Tommy has not been outside of this building since he first came here, but someone else-someone who has been outside could very easily have brought in a germ. Not only that, but germs are always in the air we breathe; all it takes are some stray germs from a cough or a sneeze, and that could cause it. We really try to keep everything sterile here, but it does not mean that germs will never get in here," explained Dr. Goldman.

Stephanie responded, "I still don't understand. I can see it if it's just something like a small head cold, but not anything that big. I know that all of you have been careful about what comes into contact with Tommy, so I just cannot see how this could have happened."

Dr. Goldman responded, "Please let me assure you; we are doing everything in our power to save Tommy and take care of him."

Stephanie boldly proclaimed, "Well my family knows someone who is all powerful and is greater than any sickness!"

Dr. Goldman nodded his head and said, "Yes, I understand. Maybe your faith will see you through this. Now, you may go in to visit Tommy if you wish, but keep it short. He is very weak, and he is very sick."

When Stephanie went into Tommy's room, she was not prepared for what she saw. Tommy looked completely different from the way that he looked the night before when she and her children visited Tommy. Tommy was asleep and looked wasted away. His breathing sounded heavy. It just wasn't the same. She just stood by him with a look of sadness and shock on her face. Stephanie began to cry a little bit, and before she left, she squeezed Tommy's hand and whispered, "I love you. We're gonna win this battle."

As Stephanie drove away from the hospital, she began to cry more. Then, a series of questions went through her mind: "Why did this happen? How could Tommy have gotten so sick, so fast? Why now, Lord? and Will there ever be an end to this?" It just didn't seem right. It just didn't seem fair.

Just then, Stephanie turned on the radio, and within seconds, the song, "His Eye Is On the Sparrow," came on. It was as if it were no coincidence that the song came on when it did. It was if the Lord knew just what she needed at that time. As the song played, God's presence and power filled the car, and God reminded her that he had not left her and forgotten her. She felt as if she had strength to go on, even though it seemed like there was no end to the difficult situation that she was in.

When she went to Anna's house to pick up her children, she told Anna about how Tommy had gotten so sick, and Anna said a prayer for Tommy. After Stephanie took her children home, had a bedtime prayer with them, and put them to bed, she called Pastor Henderson and some of her friends and told them about Tommy.

The next few days were not easy for Stephanie. Yet, she was able to look at the situation that her family was in and have the assurance that God was in control and everything was going to be alright.

On the afternoon of October 30, Stephanie was grocery shopping with her three children when she ran into Nora Wong and her two children were dressed in beautiful Chinese clothing that she had made herself, and a few people made comments on how beautiful they looked.

"Why, hello there. How have you been doing?" asked Nora.

"Well, I'm hanging in there. Tommy has gotten seriously ill with pneumonia and has gone downhill ever since. It hasn't been easy for us lately," answered Stephanie.

Nora stated, "Well, I want to let you know that I have been praying for you, and I understand what you are going through. I know that you don't know this, but my family went through something somewhat like what you are going through when my husband died from cancer a year ago. It was a hurtful experience for us, but God's grace helped me and my children get through that. We still cry over it sometimes, but God has helped us to go on and get past that."

"I never knew that," said Stephanie with surprise in her voice and in her eyes.

"I know, but I thought it would encourage you to know that," said Nora.

"Well, thank you. Hey, these are beautiful clothes. What are you so dressed up for?" asked Stephanie.

"My brother and his wife are in town. They flew in from New York City for a reunion with us, and we just came here to pick up some extra food," answered Nora.

"Well, you just go, girl! That sounds nice," said Stephanie.

Nora continued, "I have something here that I have been wanting to give to you."

Nora reached into her purse and pulled out a copy of the poem, "Footprints," and she handed it to her.

Stephanie really did not think much of it, but she said, "Thank you," and she put the poem into her purse before she went on with her shopping.

When Stephanie got home, she took out the copy of "Footprints" that Nora had given her earlier that day and read it.

After she read "Footprints," Stephanie wept for twenty minutes. In pretty much the same way that he had done it for Tommy, God showed Stephanie that he had not left her. Even though she was going through hard times and she felt like God had left her all alone, he loved her and he was there to carry her through her tough times.

Just before she stopped crying, she heard a knock on her bedroom door.

"Yes, come in," she said.

It was Billy, her youngest son.

"Mommy, why are you crying? Are you okay?" asked Billy.

Stephanie looked at Billy, smiled, and said, "It would be hard to explain it to you right now, Billy, but I'll be alright. Go to bed now."

Stephanie hugged Billy, kissed him, and sent him to bed before she went to bed herself.

A week passed, and Tommy showed little improvement. Throughout the week, Stephanie, Anna, Pastor Henderson, Carlos and Gloria, Bob and Kelly, and other people who knew about the situation with Tommy kept in touch with the hospital and prayed for Tommy.

Tommy's family had the support and prayers of the people around them, but the biggest thing that kept them going was their trust in God.

Tommy received dozens of cards and letters from people who knew about his situation, and people frequently stopped by Tommy's house and tried to minister to Stephanie and her children.

On one occasion, the Johnsons stopped by and reached out to Stephanie and her children.

Jason and Cindy played with Billy, Sally, and Michael while Bob and Kelly visited with Stephanie.

Stephanie felt blessed by their visit, and just before the Johnsons left, they all held hands and prayed for Tommy.

CHAPTER 9

The next day, Stephanie got up just like she always did before, and since it was Sunday, she thought about going to church. She did not go the week before because she was so upset about how Tommy had gotten so sick. Yet, she felt that it would be good for her to go this time.

When she and her children arrived, people greeted them, asked Stephanie about Tommy, and told her that they were praying for Tommy.

One family that she ran into was the Martinez family.

Stephanie asked them, "How is Todd? Is he still doing better?"

Carlos responded, "Yes. He is a totally new person now. He says that he is fired up for God and has even helped lead another person at the drug center to Christ."

"Well, amen!" responded Stephanie.

When Gloria asked about Tommy, Stephanie just told her, "He has made some improvement, but not enough to jump up and down and scream hallelujah about."

"Well, you just hang in there. We're all praying and believing for a miracle for Tommy. Don't you dare give up!" stated Gloria.

Stephanie and her three children sat down and waited for the service to begin. Soon after they sat down, a few more people greeted them and chatted with them. One of them was Nora Wong whom Stephanie thanked for giving her the poem, "Footprints."

Four minutes later, the service started. The congregation sang a mix of contemporary and traditional worship songs, and Stephanie felt uplifted by it. Yet, the one thing that really stood out to Stephanie and ministered to her was the song that 17-year-old Cindy Ross sang during the offering. She sang "His Eye Is On the Sparrow," and it just reminded her again of the fact that God was going to carry her and her family through her tough time.

It really looked like the whole service was meant for her when Pastor Henderson went up to the pulpit and preached a sermon titled, "The Storms of Life." It really ministered to her because it seemed to speak directly to what she was going through. Yet, it did not just speak and minister to Stephanie because there were other people like Carlos and his family who needed the message. It proved that as tough as her situation was, God had not forgotten about her and that he really truly cared about it.

After Pastor Henderson finished the message, he said, "If any of you are going through hard times now and you need someone to pray for you, then please come on down to the altars, and the altar counselors will pray for you. If you have any kinds of needs in your lives, you may also come down to the altars for prayer."

Stephanie went down to the altar, and Gina Sportelli, one of the altar counselors, prayed for her.

At the same time, the Martinez family went down to the altar for prayer. Carlos and Gloria knew that their son was doing alright then because he had accepted Christ, but they wanted to be sure he would stay on the right track. For one thing, they knew that Todd would be safe as long as he stayed at the Barnabas House, but when he came out he could have to face the temptations that got him into trouble in the first place.

For Stephanie, there was not a doubt in her mind that God had designed that service for her.

Late that afternoon, Stephanie received a phone call. It was Tommy, and Stephanie was surprised when she picked up the phone and heard Tommy's voice.

Tommy's voice sounded healthy and clear when he said, "Hi, Stephanie. I have good news for you. Not only is my pneumonia gone, but Dr. Goldman says that I have been doing so well now that I should be able to come home by Thanksgiving!"

"Praise God!" exclaimed Stephanie.

Tommy added, "I am not exactly sure of when it will be, but it should be soon."

"Well, today is November 2, so it shouldn't be too long from now. I just wish it were today! I also rejoice that you are feeling better. One week ago, you were very sick and weak, but now you sound so much better!" exclaimed Stephanie.

"Well, I have to go now. Someone just brought me dinner. I just wanted to let you know the good news. Good-bye," said Tommy.

"Good-bye," said Stephanie.

During that week, word got around about how Tommy had improved, and Tommy got visits from his family, his parents, and other people he knew, including the Johnsons.

On his way home from work, Bob stopped at the hospital, and he spent about an hour with Tommy.

When Bob got home and walked through the door, he felt pretty tired. Cindy came running up to him, sharing some things that had happened at school, but Bob calmly said, "Cindy, please, not now. I don't feel so good right now. I would love to hear what you want to tell me, but I just don't feel good right now, okay?"

Kelly added, "Daddy doesn't feel good right now, pumpkin. We need to leave him alone."

Cindy said, "Okay, but can I pray for you, Daddy?"

"Yes, that would be fine," Bob said.

Cindy closed her eyes, put her right hand on her father's arm, and prayed a prayer that went like this: "Dear Jesus, my daddy does not feel good. Please help him feel good and feel better. Amen."

As Cindy prayed for Bob, a warm feeling went from Cindy's hand into her father's body. When Cindy finished praying, Bob kissed her on the forehead and said, "Thanks honey, I feel better already. I really do mean that."

Bob's mother, Sarah, who had just come by to visit, smiled and said, "That was very sweet of you. You are really learning to be one compassionate person," and she gave her a nice hug.

"What does compassionate mean?" asked Cindy.

"It means that you care about people who are sick or having other problems," answered Cindy's grandmother as she kissed Cindy on the cheek.

CHAPTER 10

On Saturday, November 15, Stephanie went to visit Tommy at the hospital, and he told her that Dr. Goldman said that he would be able to come home from the hospital on Friday, November 21, the Friday before Thanksgiving. Stephanie rejoiced at the news, and when she went to Anna's house to pick up her two children, she told Anna and her children about it, and they rejoiced.

A few more days passed, and the big day finally came. Except for the fact that it was the Friday before Thanksgiving, it just seemed like any other day to mostly everybody else. Yet, to the Smith family, it was a very special day. A person could not walk into their home and not feel the excitement in the air.

Stephanie got up and got her children ready for school, but they all protested a little bit because they wanted to be with their father. However, Stephanie told them, "Now kids, you have to go to school. Your father should be home when you get home from school. Besides, a week from now you will have plenty of time to be with your father because you have a four-day holiday break coming.

The children reluctantly agreed, and they went to the curb to meet the school bus. After she took the children to the curb, Stephanie came home and got ready to get her husband from the hospital.

Meanwhile, Dr. Goldman met with Tommy for a few minutes that morning. He told Tommy that he would need to rest for at least a month after his release from the hospital in order to completely heal, and he told him that he needed to get an appointment set up for him in January to see his family doctor so he could tell him if he would be fit to come back to work again in January or not.

Yet, one thing that surprised Tommy was the fact that Dr. Goldman, a Jewish man, asked Tommy about his faith. It started when Dr. Goldman said, "I know and you know that I don't believe in what you believe in. Yet, I can't help but notice that you and your family really stand firm in your faith, even when you go through tough times and it is not easy to. Instead of turning away from it, you hold on tighter to it, and it gets you through."

Tommy answered, "Well, I am not going to say that it's always easy, but Jesus is the greatest thing that has happened to me and my family, and he is the one who gives us the strength to go through times like this. Without him, we probably would just have a difficult time dealing with it."

Dr. Goldman smiled, patted Tommy on the back, and said, "That's beautiful. Like I said, I don't believe in what you believe in because I am Jewish, but if your Christian faith can help your family go through something like this, that has to be good enough. Well, I have to go now. I have other patients to tend to. Your family should be here anytime now to get you. Remember, take it easy when you get home, and set up an appointment with your family doctor to see if you will be able to go back to work in January."

Dr. Goldman shook Tommy's hand and left. A half-hour later, Stephanie, Anna, and Tommy's parents were on their way to the hospital to get Tommy. Jeff and Katie, Tommy's parents, followed behind Stephanie and Anna in a separate car as they drove through Bradenton to get to the hospital. As they drove, images of Tommy's life went through Jeff's mind: images of Tommy when he first began to walk as a baby, images of Tommy playing the role of a shepherd in a Christmas play when he was seven, images of Tommy receiving an award for winning an essay contest when he was thirteen, images of Tommy graduating from high school when he was seventeen, and images Tommy getting married in 1984. He almost cried when he thought how it all led up to the things that Tommy had been going through over the past few months. Yet, God had been very faithful to him and carried him and his family through.

Nobody said much as the group entered the hospital and made the trip to Tommy's room. Yet, when they all reached Tommy's room, there was much joy and excitement in the air. Everyone hugged Tommy and told him how they were happy to see that he was finally coming home.

They all met with Dr. Goldman for a few minutes so he could explain to them how they were supposed to care for Tommy. After that came the one thing that Tommy had been waiting for-the trip back home. As they all left, a group of doctors and nurses waved to them.

Tommy rode with Stephanie and Anna, and his parents followed behind. When the car that Tommy was in came within sight of the house, it seemed as if it had been an eternity since he had been there before.

Across the street stood the Hollingsworths, another African American family that lived in Tommy's neighborhood. It had been a year and a half since they had moved to Bradenton from England, and they had come to know and love Tommy and his family very much. Nigel, Mary, and their four-year-old son, Nigel, Jr., stood and waved to Tommy as the car he was in pulled into the driveway. It was as if they all somehow knew that this was to be the day. Just as Tommy got out of the car, Nigel, Jr. ran up to Tommy and gave him a big hug. His parents came over, hugged Tommy, and briefly chatted with Tommy and his family. Later that afternoon, Tommy's children arrived, and when they saw Tommy, they all ran over to him and gave him a big hug.

They all began to overwhelm their father with stories about things that happened to them at school that day, but the one thing that stood out to Tommy was the honesty that Sally showed when she confessed to him that her excitement about her dad's coming back home had gotten her into trouble that day. That morning, she had started giggling and tickling Betsy, a friend who sat next to her during reading class when she should have been paying attention to the lesson. She had also gotten into trouble for throwing sand at two other girls on the playground.

When Sally told Tommy this, he gave her a serious look and said, "Now you know that if I am well or sick, at home or in the hospital, I expect you to behave at school-understand me?"

Sally looked at her father and nodded her head. Tommy added, "When you go to school, you go there to learn, not to play, but I do appreciate your honesty."

Throughout the afternoon, Anna, Stephanie, and Tommy's parents talked and spent time together while the children played outside.

When it was time for dinner, Stephanie, Anna, and Katie set up a nice dinner that consisted of meatloaf, rice, green beans, and salad. Stephanie called for everyone to come to the table to eat, and everyone sat down to the table.

Before everyone ate, Billy, Tommy's youngest son, said a beautiful grace that went like this: "God, thank you for this food. Please help us so it will make us strong, and thank you for bringing Daddy home. Amen."

The rest of the night, the family spent time having fellowship with each other and rejoicing over Tommy's recovery. Along with that, the family received a few phone calls from friends like Bob Johnson and Carlos Martinez, but except for that, the night was limited to them.

CHAPTER 11

The following Sunday may have seemed like any other Sunday except for the fact that it was the Sunday before Thanksgiving and something else-it was also the first Sunday that Tommy was able to join his family for church since the day he was shot.

As soon as Tommy and his family got out of their car, people loved on them by hugging them and saying things like, "How are you doing?" and "I've been praying for you." One thing that stood out to them was their seeing Todd Martinez with his family at church. From the minute they first saw him, they could tell that a great change had come into his life. He didn't look mean, vicious, or rebellious anymore. There was a glow that came from his face because Jesus had begun a new work in his life. He shook hands with Tommy and Stephanie and said, "It's just been a little while now since I have accepted Christ into my life, but it feels good! I was stubborn about living my old rebellious life, but after I thought about what happened to you, then I saw how foolish I had been. I saw how close you can come to losing your life. You can just be living your own life and minding your own business when something can happen where you lose it. It really made me look at my own life and decide it's time to straighten up."

Tommy smiled and said, "That's good. I'm glad to hear that."

Later, they ran into the Johnson family and exchanged a few loving words with them. They also ran into other people who shook hands with them, hugged them, and shared loving words with them. Some of them were people who knew Tommy and his family, and some of them were just people who did not know Tommy but knew about Tommy's situation. It didn't seem to matter to anyone, and it felt like a homecoming to Tommy.

People also reached out to the Martinez family because they knew about the situation with Todd, and they were happy to see how he had come to know Christ.

Soon after the Smiths sat down, the church service started. Right after they had the announcements, Pastor Ken Henderson asked the Smith family and the Martinez family to come to the front and give a testimony about how the Lord had taken care of them. As they came down to the front, Pastor Henderson said, "I want to tell you that both of these families have been through some fiery trials and know how faithful the Lord can be when it comes to bringing them through." Tommy said "The past six months have really been an up and down time for us, and it has not been easy. I just want to thank all of you for the love, prayers, kindness, and support that you have given to me and my family. It has truly been a touch from God."

When it was time for Carlos Martinez to speak he said, "It hasn't been easy for us either. For the past year, the devil has tried to destroy my oldest son with drugs and rebellion and tear the rest of my family apart in the process. Yet, here stands before you a testimony of how faithful God can be if you are willing to hold on and trust him. I want to thank all of you for the way that you have reached out to us during this tough time. I can also say that this has truly been a touch from God."

After church was over, more people, including Erick Gonitski and his wife, hugged the Smith family before they could leave the building.

Soon after that, a tall Portuguese man with a hearing device on hugged the Smith family and later hugged the Martinez family.

Tommy and his family all held hands as they walked to their car, and Carlos, Todd, and Calvin walked with their arms over each others' shoulders as they walked to their car with Gloria and Maria trailing behind in the same fashion.

The next day, Tommy and Stephanie woke up with a lot on their minds. They wondered about how they were going to plan for Thanksgiving, and they thought about how they were going to plan for the Christmas Holidays. Yet, the one thing that weighed the most on their minds was how they were going to pay off the $281,000 in medical bills that came from Tommy's ordeal. With Thanksgiving Day just three days away and Christmas Day and New Year's Day just around a month away, holiday plans were a big priority. Still, unknown to them, God was not finished with them yet. He was about to perform another miracle for them. Later that morning, a wealthy businessman came to the payment desk at Johnson Hospital with his 3-year-old son by the hand. It was John Waite, a 27-year-old Baptist gentleman and Seth, his 3-year-old son. On the same day that Tommy came out of the hospital, he began to sense in his heart that he ought to pay the medical bill. He had been following the situation with Tommy on the news, and it was at this point that he wanted to pay off the bill. With his salary as a businessman, he had the means to do it, and that is why he felt that way. As he stood there to pay the bill, his 3-year-old son stood there and waited patiently.

Three days later, it was Thanksgiving Day, and Tommy's immediate family, and Anna, Jeff and Katie were all sitting down, eating Thanksgiving dinner. They were all eating, talking, and sharing time together when the telephone rang. It was Ken Henderson, the pastor. When Tommy answered the phone, Ken Henderson said, "I apologise if I cut in when you were eating. I just wanted to call and say, "Holiday Blessings and Happy Thanksgiving." You are such a blessing to us."

Tommy responded, "Well, thank you. You're a blessing to us."

After Tommy hung up the phone, Stephanie asked, "Who was that, dear?"

Tommy responded, "It was the pastor. He just wanted to say 'Happy Thanksgiving and Holiday Blessings' and tell me how much everyone appreciates me at church."

"That's nice, honey," said Stephanie.

Later that afternoon, Stephanie and Anna were taking a walk around the block and talking about the situation with Tommy when they ran into Sue Mays, a woman whom Stephanie had known since seventh grade. They stopped and chatted a little bit about what happened to Tommy. It was a friendly conversation until Sue Mays began to put Tommy down. She said, "You know, I don't mean to sound mean or rude, but I don't know why you even married such a person in the first place."

Stephanie frowned and asked, "What do you mean?"

Sue continued, "Well, he seems so different. I see him as rather nerdy. Back in high school he was always the nobody type of person who didn't fit in. He was never really popular, and some people thought he was goofy. I always thought that you could do better than marrying someone like that."

Anna frowned, and Stephanie, a person who was usually not outspoken, said, "You know, I think you are wrong. Tommy may not appeal to you, but to me he is the best husband in the world! He may seem like a total outcast to you, but I have found him to be a loving, gentle, caring person. Maybe he's not good enough for you, but he treats me with respect and treats me like a woman. I think that that is what really counts!"

Sue just turned and walked away with an attitude.

Anna turned to Stephanie and said, "I can't believe the nerve of that woman! How can she always say such awful things about people?"

Stephanie responded, "Well, I have always known her to be outspoken about what she thinks and feels, and even rude with it sometimes. Still, I am shocked that she would say such things about my husband. I have known her since I was in seventh grade."

That night, the family gathered together again for some pumpkin pie, hot chocolate, and fellowship. They also spent time discussing God's goodness and how he had brought them through the tough times that they had been through. "I just don't know how we could have done it without Jesus," said Tommy's father with a tear in his voice.

"Amen," said Stephanie.

The next day, Carlos called Tommy to see if he felt like going out with him just for the ride as he took care of some errands. Tommy told him that he did feel like doing that, and Carlos took him with him.

They were on their way from the bank when Tommy asked if they could stop by the hospital to see if there was anything that he could do about the big hospital bill that came from his getting shot. Yet, when they got to the hospital and reached the payment desk, they had an unexpected surprise. The lady at the front desk said, "Oh, we forgot to call you and tell you that the bill has been taken care of. On Monday morning, a wealthy young man came and paid off your hospital bill. You don't owe us anything! It was an anonymous person who said that he knew about your situation and that he wanted to help."

Tommy and Carlos smiled, laughed, and hugged each other after they heard the good news. The lady at the front desk smiled. It was true. Once again, God had come through by making a way for him and his family. In his own special way, God had provided another touch from God. Tommy called his wife over the phone to tell her the good news, and she rejoiced over the phone.

On the way home, Carlos stopped at a toy store to buy a doll for his daughter for Christmas. Carlos and Tommy ran into Kelly Johnson and her two children and chatted briefly with them. Just as Carlos and Tommy were getting into the car to leave, a homeless man rode up to them on a raggedy old bicycle and asked them for money for cigarettes.

Tommy responded, "Look mister. We can help you out if you need food. I'll gladly buy you something to eat, but I don't want to help you get something that will ruin your health."

The man responded, "Well, I am hungry, and there's a McDonald's just down the street. Could you please get me something to eat? C'mon, you can trust me. I can just ride on over on my bike if you drive over there. Please, could you?"

Carlos drove to the McDonald's and the man rode his bike to it. Tommy went inside and bought the man something to eat while Carlos briefly talked with the man about the Lord, but Tommy had to wait in line for five minutes because a crowd of hungry people who had been Christmas shopping stopped in for lunch and crowded the restaurant. When Tommy came out with the food, the man's face lit up and he said, "You didn't just ride off and leave me here with nothing to eat- you kept your word!"

Tommy gave the man a Gospel leaflet and briefly told the man that God loves him and wants to come into his life. The man said, "After what you did for me, I think that there must really be something to this Jesus. You didn't just preach at me-you put your faith into action by meeting my need."

The next day, the Smiths had an unexpected visitor at their home. It was Thomas Dawson, a tall, thin, long-haired man whom Tommy had led to Christ a year before that. He used a lot of hip talk, and it made Tommy and his family chuckle to hear it. When Tommy answered the doorbell and opened the door, Thomas hugged Tommy and said, "Hey dude, remember me? I just thought that I would cruise on by and check on ya. I know that you've been through a pretty hairy situation and thought that I would see how you've been doing."

"Well thanks," said Tommy.

"Have you been doin' alright?" asked the man.

"Yes," answered Tommy.

As Thomas spoke, Tommy's three children who were on the floor while they watched a Christmas cartoon video looked up and smiled, and Stephanie covered her face to hide her laughter as she walked out of the family room.

Before Thomas left, he hugged Tommy again and said, "I love ya. Check ya later dude. I am gonna hop on my cycle and cruise now, but I thought I would come by and see about you," and he left.

The following Monday, Tommy's family attended a party at a recreation center in Bradenton. At the party, they were reunited with the people who were involved in saving Tommy's life on the day he was shot. Many of the people whom Tommy and his family knew were there, including children and parents from the school where Tommy worked, and friends from church. Mr. Brown, the man whom Tommy had gone to see on the day he was shot, shook Tommy's hand and gave him a hug. It was the first time since the shooting that he got to see Tommy since he was so ill himself. Tommy and Stephanie let him know that he should not feel guilty for the shooting.

A little while later, Tommy made a short speech in which he said, "I just want to thank all of you for what you did for me. I want to thank all of the people who prayed for me. I also want to say that if it weren't for my family's Christian faith and trust in God, we would not have made it. God is the one who deserves the credit for healing me, and he is the one who really saw us through the whole thing. If any of you out there do not know Jesus, we invite you to accept him and let him come into your life like we did."

When it was Stephanie's turn to speak, she just said, "Ditto," and everybody laughed and clapped.

The family got back in late that night. As soon as they got home, they prayed with their children and put them to bed. After the children were in bed, Stephanie stayed with them a little longer, and Billy, their youngest son, asked, "Mommy how can Jesus make sick people well again?"

Stephanie answered, "I really don't know, honey, but he does. I don't even know the answer to that, but I do know that he is very good and has all of the power in the world. So if he is willing to do it, he can heal people like Daddy and make them well again-even if it's too hard for the doctors to do it. Sometimes he does it, but sometimes for some reason he does not do it. Fortunately for us, this time he did heal Daddy."

Billy smiled and said, "He's like a really very powerful doctor, isn't he?"

"Yes, dear. Now you need your rest. Go to sleep now," said Stephanie.

A few minutes after Stephanie joined Tommy in bed, Stephanie began to cry, and Tommy asked her, "What's wrong?"

Stephanie replied, "Well, it's no big deal. It's just that when I think of everything that we've been through and how faithful and good that God has been to us, I get emotional."

Tommy responded, "I see."

Then, Tommy kissed her.

Stephanie smiled and said, "You are so sweet."

Soon after that, they both fell asleep.

From the Author

I hope that A Touch From God has touched your heart and ministered to you. I don't know what you have been going through or what you have been dealing with in your life, but God does. Maybe you haven't had to face anything like the Martinez family or the Smith family had to face, but God cares about your needs, and he wants to minister to those needs. He may not do it in the way that you want him to, but he wants to help you.

What's even more important is the fact that God wants to forgive you for your sins and come into your heart and life. You can do that now by praying a prayer like the following prayer:

Dear Father God, I am sorry for my sins. I believe that Jesus died on the cross for my sins, and by faith I accept him into my heart and life as my lord and my savior. Please help me to live for you each day. In Jesus's name I pray, amen.

If you prayed that prayer right now and meant it from your heart, Jesus is in your heart and life right now, and you can be sure that he will help you to be a better person in this life and give you an eternal home in heaven.

PLEASE NOTE

All of the scriptures that I used in A Touch From God were from the King James Version of the Bible, and I used the McDonalds trademark name with their permission.